S

That Mushy Stuff

YEARLING BOOKS are designed especially to entertain and enlighten young people. Patricia Reilly Giff, consultant to this series, received her bachelor's degree from Marymount College and a master's degree in history from St. John's University. She holds a Professional Diploma in Reading and a Doctorate of Humane Letters from Hofstra University. She was a teacher and reading consultant for many years, and is the author of numerous books for young readers.

That Mushy Stuff

JUDY DELTON

Illustrated by Alan Tiegreen

A YEARLING BOOK

Published by
Bantam Doubleday Dell Books for Young Readers
a division of
Bantam Doubleday Dell Publishing Group, Inc.
1540 Broadway
New York, New York 10036

ISBN: 0-440-40176-3

Printed in the United States of America

February 1989

30 29 28 27 26 25 24 23 22 21

CWO

For Smokeless Dort, a badge for you.
Now we can share the Best-Buy view.

Contents

CHAPTER 1

Frostbite and Nosebleeds

Hearts, hearts, hearts. Mrs. Peters's dining room was filled with red hearts.

"Valentines!" shouted Molly Duff.

You could make valentines. And you could be a valentine.

Patty Baker was Roger White's valentine. But Molly didn't have a valentine. Yet.

Mrs'. Peters smiled. "Soon it will be

February. The month for valentines," she said. "But we won't make valentines today. Today we will learn how to earn our first-aid badges."

Molly sat up to listen. She loved to earn badges. All of the Pee Wee Scouts loved new badges. Even more than valentines!

Molly wondered what the first-aid badge would look like. Maybe it would have a Band-Aid on it. Molly liked Band-Aids. Especially the ones with pictures of clowns on them.

Mrs. Peters had a first-aid kit in front of her on the table. She was their troop leader. Their Pee Wee Scout Troop 23 leader.

"You can make your first-aid kit with some things from home," she said. "You'll need a cigar box or a small shoe box."

Mrs. Peters passed out papers. The

papers said what the Scouts should put
into their first-aid kits:

Band-Aids   Adhesive tape
Bandages   Clean cloth
Scissors   First-aid book
Calamine lotion   Soap

3

Needles and	Matches
safety pins	Phone numbers and
	money for calls

"My mom won't let me have matches," said Sonny Betz. "Or a scissors either."

Could Sonny be my valentine? Molly wondered. No. Sonny was a baby. Not a boyfriend.

"This isn't to play with, Sonny," said Mrs. Peters. "This is to help people."

"We have all this stuff at home," said Kevin Moe. "I won't have to buy any-thing."

"We do too," said Rachel Meyers. "My dad is a dentist."

"Ho, ho, Rachel's dad puts Band-Aids on his teeth!" shouted Roger.

"He does not," said Rachel crossly. "He's just like a doctor. His name is Dr.

Meyers. He can fix other things besides teeth."

"Cannot," said Roger.

"Can too," said Rachel.

Mrs. Peters held up her hand for quiet. Then she told Troop 23 what all the things were used for.

"To get the badge," she said, "you must make a small kit of your own. And you must give someone emergency help. For instance, if your little sister falls down on the sidewalk, you could wash her knee and put on a Band-Aid. Today we will talk about other emergencies too."

"What if we fall down ourselves?" asked Tracy Barnes. "Can we give first aid to ourselves?"

Mrs. Peters thought about that. "Yes," she said, "but it is a Scout's duty to help others. So for this badge you must also give aid to someone else."

"I don't have any brothers or sisters," said Rachel, pouting.

"I do," said Mary Beth Kelly. "My little brothers are always falling down."

Molly groaned. Mary Beth would get her first-aid badge fast.

"There are other emergencies too," Mrs. Peters went on. "If someone burns himself on something hot, the first thing to do is to put ice on the burn. Then you find an adult to help."

Molly tried to think of someone she could help who got burned. Her mother wouldn't let her use the stove alone. And she never got near any fires.

This might be a hard badge to earn!

"Now, if a dog bites someone, and no

one is nearby, what would you do?" asked Mrs. Peters.

"I'd run away fast, so I wouldn't get bit," said Tim Noon.

The Pee Wees laughed.

"But what would you do to help the victim?" asked Mrs. Peters.

"Put a Band-Aid on the bite?" said Patty Baker. She was Kenny Baker's twin sister.

"That's close," said Mrs. Peters. "First you must wash the wound with soap and water. Then rinse it and dry it with a clean towel. Then put on the bandage. And then call an adult so the person can get to the doctor. Dog bites can be dangerous."

"Lucky wouldn't bite anyone," said Roger, patting Lucky on the head. Lucky was their mascot.

"Tiny wouldn't either!" said Tracy. Tiny

was Mrs. Peters's dog. They both came to all the Scout meetings.

"But some dogs do bite," said Mrs. Peters. "And some dogs have rabies."

"Arf!" said Lucky.

"He doesn't have rabies," said Tim.

Then Mrs. Peters told the Pee Wees what to do for nosebleeds. "Put the victim's head back," she said, "and hold the nose for ten minutes. Then put a cold towel on the nose."

All the Scouts held their noses. When they talked their voices sounded funny.

Mrs. Peters had to hold up her hand again. When they were quiet, she talked about frostbite. And broken bones. She showed them how to make a stretcher out of coats. "Never let a victim walk if a leg is painful or broken," she said.

"And if you are at a picnic or barbecue

and anyone's clothes catch fire, the victim should roll on the grass. Or be wrapped in a blanket until the flames go out. Then of course he or she must get to the doctor right away."

Lisa Ronning was waving her hand.

"Once the meat on our barbecue caught fire," she said.

"Did you wrap it in a blanket?" said Roger. He laughed.

Mrs. Peters frowned. "Barbecues can be very dangerous," she said. "Especially for small children."

"Smarty-pants," said Lisa to Roger.

Mrs. Peters passed out little first-aid books to the Scouts for their kits.

"Read these now," she said. "And put your first-aid kit together as soon as you can. Then help someone in an emergency. And you will earn your badge."

The meeting was almost over. The Pee Wees told one another some good deeds they had done that week. They sang the Pee Wee Scout song. They said the Pee Wee Scout pledge.

But all Molly could think about was

how she would find an emergency. Her mom was a very careful person. She did not leave matches around. And Molly had no little brothers or sisters to scrape their knees, like Tracy and Mary Beth did. It wasn't fair! Everyone else would get their badges before she did.

Before the Pee Wees left, Mrs. Peters's baby Nick woke up. All the Scouts ran to see him. He was just two months old.

Molly loved him. But even Nick could not interest Molly today. She had to find an emergency. Molly wanted to be the first one to earn a first-aid badge.

CHAPTER 2

Looking for an Emergency

All week long the Pee Wee Scouts watched for emergencies. Roger and Patty watched together. They were together all the time.

Everyone had their first-aid kits ready. All the items on the list. But Sonny didn't have matches in his kit. His mother had said no.

Every day after school, Molly and Lisa

got together to watch for injured people. They carried their kits with them wherever they went.

"There are no barbecues in winter," Lisa complained. "How can we roll someone on the grass if it is all covered with snow?"

"We have to find some winter emergencies," said Molly. "Like frostbite."

The girls watched the people walking by. They had rosy faces. They looked cold.

"That lady looks like she has frostbite," whispered Lisa. She pointed.

Molly shook her head. "Her face is rosy. Mrs. Peters said your skin turns white. And your fingers get numb. Or your toes."

A man came by with a cane. He was walking very slowly. Maybe his toes were cold.

"His face isn't rosy!" said Lisa. "And he

hasn't got any gloves on. I'll bet his fingers are frozen."

"What do we do?" asked Molly.

"We say, 'Pardon me, sir, but are your fingers numb?' " said Lisa.

"He might get mad," said Molly. "He might hit me with his cane."

While the girls wondered what to do, the man walked past them, down the street.

"This first-aid badge is going to be the hardest one to get." Lisa sighed.

"Tracy already bandaged her little sister's hand," said Molly. "Tracy said she cut it on a toy and there was real blood. Lots of it."

Lisa sighed again.

Lucky Tracy, thought Molly. She had a big family. Someone was bound to get hurt.

What Molly needed was a bigger family. Or at least a mom who was careless.

"Let's look for dogs that might bite," said Lisa. "In the park."

But all the dogs in the park were on leashes. They looked happy. They didn't look like they wanted to bite anyone.

"Cats scratch," said Lisa. "But I don't know where there are any."

The girls walked around the block looking for speeding cars and children on skateboards. They looked for fires and accidents and someone who might have a nosebleed. But everyone looked very healthy.

"I'm going home," said Lisa. "I'll see you tomorrow."

Molly waved and went back to her own house. She sat and read her first-aid book.

When her mom said, "Ouch!" Molly ran

with her kit. But Mrs. Duff had just stubbed her toe.

When her dad coughed, Molly ran to see if he had choked on the potato chip he was eating. But he had stopped coughing by the time she got there.

All week Molly listened and watched.

All week Molly and Lisa could not find a single emergency.

On Tuesday the Pee Wee Scouts met again.

"I bandaged my little sister's knee," said Tracy as soon as they got there.

"My dad cut himself shaving," said Kenny. "I got the alcohol to put on it."

Show-offs, thought Molly.

"My little brother bumped his head on the kitchen table," said Mary Beth. "I put ice on it and it didn't swell up."

"What good Pee Wees you are in an emergency!" said Mrs. Peters. "I am so proud of you."

Not of me, thought Molly. How did those Scouts find all these victims? Molly's dad never cut himself shaving. Never, ever. Molly felt upset with her family. Would she be the only one without a first-aid badge?

Mrs. Peters called the Scouts' names for their badges.

Boring, thought Molly.

Boring not to get a badge.

"Tracy Barnes," called Mrs. Peters. Tracy walked up to the front of the room, and Mrs. Peters pinned a big round badge right on her blouse! It was light blue, and it said FIRST AID around the edge. In a circle. In the very middle was a bright red cross.

Molly wanted one of those badges more

than anything in the world. She felt like grabbing it off Tracy's blouse and putting it on her own!

Mary Beth and Kenny went up for their badges. Molly tried to pretend she didn't care. She hummed a song and played with Lucky.

But inside her head, she had a plan. A plan to help her get that blue badge with the red cross soon. And she wasn't going to tell her plan to anyone. It was a secret plan!

CHAPTER 3

A Boyfriend for Molly

At the next Scout meeting, Mrs. Peters did not talk about badges. Or first aid. She said, "Today we are going to think about valentines."

Molly was glad. That would give her more time to think about her secret plan. She needed time. Her plan wasn't easy.

"I love valentines!" said Rachel. "Once in first grade I got candy from a boy who liked me. My mom called him my little Prince Charming."

"Valentines usually mean romance," said Mrs. Peters, smiling.

The Pee Wees giggled. Romance was funny.

They all pointed to Roger and Patty. Roger's face turned red.

"But hearts are also a part of the body," Mrs. Peters went on, "and some things are not good for hearts. Do you know what they are?" she asked.

"Scaring people," said Sonny. "My mom says I shouldn't scare my grandma or I'll give her a heart attack."

"Boo!" shouted Roger.

"Boo yourself!" said Sonny.

Soon all the Pee Wees were scaring one another.

"Something else that isn't good for

hearts," said Mrs. Peters, "is smoking. Mr. Phipps at the bank downtown has asked all the Scouts in town to make valentines to hang in his bank. I thought Troop 23's valentines could remind people that smoke is bad for the heart. And you can make other valentines for your friends," she said.

"My aunt smokes," said Tim.

"So does my cousin," said Kevin.

"Then you might make valentines for them too," said Mrs. Peters.

She passed out some lacy white paper and some red paper. And scissors and crayons and paste.

"Now, let's all think before we start," said Mrs. Peters.

Molly wanted to start her two valentines right now. She hated to think. She wanted to get right at the lacy paper.

Cut, cut, cut.

Fold, fold, fold.

Molly loved to make things and decorate them. Her mom said she was very creative.

"Let's talk about what we will write on our no-smoking valentines," said Mrs. Peters.

The Pee Wees put their chins in their hands and pretended to think.

Hmmm.

Think, think, think.

All of a sudden Rachel waved her hand. "Smoke is no joke," she said.

"That's a very good motto, Rachel," said Mrs. Peters. "It's nice and short so people will remember it."

Why didn't I think of that? thought Molly. She had to think of one just as good! But now she couldn't be first.

Not first with a motto.

Not first with first aid.

"Can we use Rachel's motto, Mrs. Peters?" asked Lisa.

"Well, I think each saying should be

different," said Mrs. Peters. "Next week will be almost Valentine's Day. You can think about it at home this week. Today we will make the valentines. We can write in them later. We will each make one for a friend. And one to hang in the bank."

Rat's knees, thought Molly. Now she had two things to worry about instead of one.

The Pee Wees cut and pasted valentines the whole rest of the meeting.

"Roger's making one for Patty," whispered Mary Beth. "I saw her name on it."

Of course, thought Molly. She was his girlfriend. Molly made her no-smoking valentine first. She left it blank inside.

Who should be her valentine?

She didn't have a boyfriend. She had already made one for her mom and dad, in school. She wished she had someone special. Her own valentine.

Patty was working hard on a big card in the shape of a baseball. Molly knew it was for Roger.

Suddenly Molly had an idea. She would make a valentine for Sonny. Even if he was a baby. Molly felt sorry for Sonny. Everyone laughed at him because he was a baby. Poor Sonny. It was no fun to be picked on.

Molly made up her mind.

She would be Sonny's girlfriend!

CHAPTER 4

Don't Smoke in the Tub

By the end of the meeting Molly's valentine was finished. It was beautiful. It had a picture of a dog on it. Sonny liked dogs. And it had lots of hearts and flowers.

Inside, Molly wrote, *Be my valentine. I love you. Molly D.* She slipped her valentine into Sonny's book bag.

The Scouts cleaned up the paper.

Then they told their good deeds. They

sang their Pee Wee Scout song and said their Pee Wee Scout pledge.

On the way home, Roger handed his valentine to Patty. Patty opened the card shyly. It had a picture of a boy with a bat in his hand. It said, *I'd go to bat for you, Valentine.*

"I read that on a valentine at the drugstore," said Roger proudly.

Inside the valentine were four baseball cards.

Patty turned bright red. As red as the hearts on the card. She really is shy, thought Molly.

What could Molly give Sonny? If Roger gave Patty his baseball cards, he really must like her. She had to find something to give Sonny. Or something to do for him.

Molly had too much to think about. Her

head ached from thinking. When she got home, she went to her room and sat down.

She tried to write a no-smoking saying. She thought and thought. "Rat's knees," Molly said. She thought some more. Smoke. Croak. Don't smoke or you will croak!

No, that was not a nice thing to tell people. She didn't think Mrs. Peters would like it.

Molly threw herself on her bed and fell asleep. She was tired from thinking so hard.

The next day, on the playground, Roger slipped a Twinkie in Patty's coat pocket. And when they went into school, he put a ballpoint pen on her desk. During math, Roger just sat and stared at Patty.

"I wish someone would stare at me,"

said Molly to Mary Beth at recess. Sonny hadn't said one word about Molly's valentine.

"We're too young to have boyfriends. My mom says so," said Mary Beth.

"I don't care," said Molly. "I want one."

She was not going to give up on Sonny. She would get him. But she wouldn't tell anyone. Not even Mary Beth.

After recess, Molly noticed something white on her desk. It was an envelope. When she opened it, a heart-shaped valentine fell out. It did not have a name on it. It just said, *From your secret valentine.*

Molly was glad to get a valentine. But who had given it to her?

After school Roger grabbed Patty's books and carried them for her. Patty turned red again.

Molly tried to grab Sonny's book bag, but he pushed her away and ran off down the street.

"Do you like Roger?" whispered Molly in Patty's ear.

"He's all right," said Patty shyly.

All right! The cutest, tallest boy in the second grade liked Patty, and all she said was all right!

Molly would have thrown her arms around Roger's neck and hugged him.

Maybe even given him a kiss like they did on TV. Smack, smack, smack.

The next morning there was a new pencil on Patty's desk. And an eraser in the shape of Big Bird. She put them into her desk.

On Molly's desk was another envelope!

She tore it open. It said, *From your secret valentine.* Again! Who could it be? She looked at Sonny. He was chewing on his pencil. He didn't look like a secret valentine to Molly.

The week was going by fast. Molly did not have a smoking verse. And she did not have a first-aid badge. She did not have a boyfriend either.

She ran home from school and wrote down all the words that rhymed with smoke. *Coke. Folk. Poke. Soak. Woke. Yolk.*

Maybe she should turn the rhyme around. She wrote, *Rub a dub dub, don't smoke in the tub.* That was good! But only for people who smoked in the bathtub. Lots of people smoked in their cars. Or while watching TV. What about those people?

"Rat's knees!" said Molly. She stamped her foot.

She couldn't give up. She would be the only one without a valentine to hang in the bank. People would say, "Where is Molly Duff's? Isn't she a Pee Wee Scout? Maybe she wasn't smart enough to make one."

Cigarettes are bad.
No smoking, Dad.

But Molly's dad didn't smoke. No good.

Help your heart, please don't puff.
Help your heart, says Molly Duff.

There! That was just right. People who read it would know Molly wrote it.

Now, if she could just think of a way to make Sonny her boyfriend. Or was he her valentine already? Her secret valentine.

CHAPTER **5**

Sonny Slides Away

It was cold the next morning. February was a cold month. On the way to school, Tracy and Mary Beth wore their first-aid badges on the outside of their jackets.

That is just to make me jealous, said Molly to herself. The first-aid badge seemed bigger than the other badges. And brighter.

The girls met the other Pee Wee Scouts

on the corner. Patty was running and sliding on the ice. Roger and Tim ran behind her, sliding and slipping.

"Whooa!" shouted Kevin, sliding farther than any of them.

"I can slide farther than that!" shouted Sonny. He got a running start. He bent over like a racer and shot toward the icy strip of sidewalk. "Look at me!" he called.

Just as he said that, Molly bent down to brush some dirt off her boot.

Smack! Sonny slid right into Molly. He went down on the ice.

"You tripped me!" Sonny shouted. "Oooo, my head."

"It was an accident," said Molly.

Sonny lay on the sidewalk with his arms and legs out like a snow angel. The other Scouts kept sliding around. But Molly and Lisa stayed near Sonny.

"He hit his head!" shouted Molly. "Get some ice!"

"I don't want any more ice," wailed Sonny.

But Lisa was busy packing snow into hard balls to put on Sonny's head. "This will keep it from swelling," she said.

"You need first aid," said Molly.

"I don't want first aid!" shouted Sonny, struggling to push Lisa and Molly away. "You tripped me on purpose."

Sonny's mittens had fallen off. His hands looked cold and white.

"I think he's got frostbite!" said Molly. She jumped up and down with excitement. She looked in her first-aid book to see what to do.

"Is anything broken?" asked Lisa.

Sonny sat up in the snow. "Just my lunch box," he said.

"Dummy," said Molly, "we don't give first aid to lunch boxes."

"You have to buy me a new one," said Sonny. "You broke it."

The other Pee Wee Scouts gathered around to watch the first aid. Soon they were as excited as Lisa and Molly.

"We need a stretcher!" shouted Kevin, taking charge. He took off his jacket and began to make a stretcher the way Mrs. Peters had shown them.

"He's *our* victim," shouted Molly, stamping her foot. "Get out of here!"

But Kevin did not have his badge yet either. He wasn't going to leave when he could see a perfectly good chance to earn a badge.

"Give me another coat," he ordered, grabbing Tim's jacket by the sleeves.

"Hey, I'm cold!" said Tim. But Kevin

grabbed Tim's coat anyway. He tied the sleeves together. He pulled the two jackets under Sonny.

"Hey, quit it," said Sonny. "I'm fine."

Sonny didn't want to be a victim. But every time he tried to get to his feet, one of the Pee Wees pushed him back onto the stretcher.

"Get down," said Kevin, giving Sonny a shove.

Lisa put more snow on his head.

Molly put Sonny's mittens back on his hands. "He has to be warm because of the frostbite," she said.

The Scouts started carrying Sonny down the street toward his house.

"I'm going to school!" he shouted.

"You can't!" Molly shouted back.

She took her bandage roll from her kit

and started to bandage Sonny's head. "Lie still!" she said. "Rat's knees, you're hard to help."

"His knee is bleeding," said Lisa.

"Really?" said Molly.

Sure enough, there was a hole in the knee of Sonny's pants. He had scraped his knee on the ice.

"BLOOD!" shouted Molly. "Oh, boy. Blood!" She jumped up and down. This was no game. This was real first aid!

Her secret plan was working better than ever.

Patty got some antiseptic lotion out of her kit and put it on Sonny's knee. Molly popped a Band-Aid with a clown on it over the scrape.

"I don't see any blood," said Kevin, looking over Molly's shoulder.

"There wasn't much, but it was there," Molly said.

Kevin smiled at her.

"We could have put one of those tourniquet things on his leg if there was more blood," said Lisa. "Oh, well. Maybe next time."

The Scouts dragged Sonny along on the coats through the snow.

"I'm going to be late for school," he said.

"We all are," said Roger. "But this is important."

Suddenly Sonny jerked forward and jumped off the coats. He dashed down the street toward school.

"Get him!" screamed Molly.

The Scouts chased Sonny, but he had a head start. And he was a fast runner. The Pee Wees let him go.

Tim and Kevin untied their jackets and put them back on.

"Oh, no!" cried Molly. "Our only victim and he got away. How will I get my first-aid badge now?"

CHAPTER 6

The Big Blue Badge

All day Molly felt bad for tripping Sonny. She did need to get that badge, but that was no way to treat a boyfriend.

The next morning she waited outside of Sonny's house. When he came out, she said, "I'll carry your books to school." She had her hopes up.

But Sonny said, "Why? I can carry my books myself."

Molly grabbed Sonny's book bag.

Sonny grabbed it back.

"Get out of here!" he yelled. "Just leave me alone!"

Having a boyfriend is hard work, thought Molly.

Sonny ran all the way to school.

"Wait!" Molly shouted. She chased him every step of the way.

After school, Molly was the first Pee Wee Scout out of the classroom at three o'clock. She was the first onto the bus. The big bus that took the Pee Wee Scouts to Mrs. Peters's house.

Molly had her valentine ready.

But Mrs. Peters held up some badges. First-aid badges!

"Some people do not have their first-aid badges," she said.

"I do," said Tracy.

"Are there any others who have earned their badge this week?" Mrs. Peters asked.

Molly waved her hand. So did Lisa and Kevin and some of the other Scouts.

"We saved Sonny's life," said Lisa. "He fell on the ice and hit his head and his knee was bleeding and he had frostbite."

"We were the only ones around," said Kevin. "It was definitely an emergency."

"But he got away," said Molly, not wanting to lie about something as important as a Scout badge. "Can we get a badge if the victim jumps off the stretcher?" she asked anxiously.

"We put ice on the bump on his head," said Lisa.

"We made a stretcher in case anything was broken," said Kevin.

"It wasn't!" said Sonny. "I wasn't even hurt. And Molly tripped me."

"Liar!" shouted Kevin. "You were too hurt! Your knee had real blood on it!"

"We bandaged his knee," said Molly. "Patty put lotion on it because we didn't have soap and water to wash it."

"Well, it sounds like you did a good job," said Mrs. Peters. "And you surely deserve a first-aid badge. You may have prevented an infection in Sonny's knee."

"And a bump on his head," said Kevin.

"I wasn't even hurt," Sonny muttered again.

"Well, you all acted wisely," said Mrs. Peters. Then she called out the names of the people who had helped.

Molly and Lisa were first! Molly had her new badge at last. Her big blue badge.

Lisa pinned hers on her blouse.

Molly pinned hers on her sweater.

"This was the hardest badge I ever earned in my life," said Lisa.

If it wasn't for my plan, thought Molly, we still wouldn't have it. But she didn't tell anyone. Not even Lisa.

Just then Nick woke up. Mrs. Peters brought him out for the Scouts to see.

"Look at him smile!" said Rachel.

"In a few months, he'll have a tooth to show you," said Mrs. Peters proudly. "His very first tooth."

All the Pee Wees gathered around Nick to look in his mouth. But there were no teeth yet. Not even one little white tooth.

"Then he'll be able to eat sandwiches," said Roger. "Like regular people."

"Silly," said Rachel. "Babies eat baby food even when they have teeth."

But Roger didn't snap back at Rachel

today. He was in a good mood. It was almost Valentine's Day. And his valentine was Patty.

Molly used a little glue and stuck a big red heart on the back of Sonny's shirt. It said, *Molly and Sonny.*

The Pee Wees pointed to it and laughed. "Sonny's got a girlfriend," they sang.

Patty was glad that the Scouts were teasing somebody else for once.

Sonny looked mad. When he found the sign on his back, he tore it up into pieces.

Mrs. Peters put Nick down in his crib and said, "Let's hear the no-smoking valentines. Who wants to read theirs first?"

"I read mine last week, Mrs. Peters," said Rachel loudly.

"That's right, I remember," Mrs. Peters said.

Molly waved her hand.

"Molly," said Mrs. Peters, "read yours first."

Help your heart, don't puff.
Help your heart, says Molly Duff.

Mrs. Peters clapped. "That is wonderful!" she said. "Who would like to be next?"

"Happy Valentine's Day to my heart!" read Tracy.

Mrs. Peters clapped again.

Kevin read,

> *Healthy heart, healthy heart,*
> *Put out that weed and do your part.*

"A weed is a dandelion," said Sonny. "That's dumb."

"A weed is a cigarette," said Kevin. "My dad said so."

"Tim, do you have a saying?" asked Mrs. Peters.

Tim stood up and read, "Don't smoke."

The Scouts laughed.

"I can't write poems," said Tim. His face turned red.

"That's fine," said Mrs. Peters. "It's short and to the point."

"Now," she went on, "we will write our sayings neatly in our valentines. Then we'll go off to the bank and hang them up."

"I love banks," said Kevin. "Can we get some money there?"

Mrs. Peters laughed. "I don't think so, but maybe we'll get lollipops."

"Yum!" said Tim.

"Now," said Mrs. Peters, "the bank has a community bulletin board. While people wait in line for the tellers, they can read our messages."

Soon all the Scouts had finished writing their valentines.

"Let's go!" shouted Roger.

"Yeah," said Molly, "let's go to the bank!"

CHAPTER 7

The Real Valentine

Mrs. Peters dressed Nick and put him in his car seat. Then all the Scouts piled into Mrs. Peters's new van. It was crowded when all eleven Pee Wee Scouts were inside. Roger pulled Patty down on his lap to make more room. She turned red again.

Molly tried to pull Sonny down on her lap.

56

"Hey, cut it out!" Sonny yelled. "I hate that mushy stuff."

"Molly's got a boyfriend," sang Tracy.

Molly only wished it were true. She wouldn't mind being teased. But she didn't have a boyfriend. Sonny was a pain in the neck. For someone who had sent her two secret valentines, he wasn't very friendly!

Maybe it wasn't Sonny. Who could it be?

At the bank, the president, Mr. Phipps, came out of his office. He welcomed the Pee Wee Scouts of Troop 23. He showed them a nice big bulletin board near the bank tellers. He gave Mrs. Peters a box of thumbtacks.

Each Pee Wee Scout troop had its own part of the bulletin board.

Troop 23 got to work. They hung up all their no-smoking valentines.

"Those are good valentine messages," said Mr. Phipps. "I just quit smoking this month."

"Your heart will thank you," said Kevin.

"That's true, young man," said Mr. Phipps with a smile.

Molly noticed that Roger hung his valentine next to Patty's. Molly's was between Mary Beth's and Kevin's.

Mr. Phipps took a picture of all the Pee Wee Scouts lined up in front of their valentines. "I'll put the picture at the top," he said. Then he thanked them for coming to the bank. He gave each Scout a lollipop.

The Pee Wees piled into the van and went back to Mrs. Peters's house.

The Scouts told some good deeds they had done that week.

"I helped my grandma roll up her knitting yarn," said Lisa.

"I gave our dog a bath," said Tim. "And he wouldn't hold still."

"Those are very good deeds," said Mrs. Peters. "Anyone else?"

"I gave Patty a Big Bird eraser," said Roger.

"That's not a good deed," said Kevin. "That's because she's your girlfriend."

"It is too a good deed," said Roger. He smiled at Patty.

"Roger's a pest," said Kenny. "I think he should leave my sister alone."

"Says who?" said Roger.

Kenny put his fists up. "You leave Patty alone."

"Wanna fight?" said Roger. "I'll fight for Patty."

"Molly's a pest too!" shouted Sonny. "Give her a punch for me."

All the Pee Wees began to shout.

Mrs. Peters held up her hand for silence. "We'll sing our song now, and say our pledge. Everyone calm down, please."

The Pee Wee Scouts joined hands in a

60

big circle. Roger held one of Patty's hands and Kenny held the other.

Molly grabbed Sonny's hand. He yanked it away.

"Why won't you be my boyfriend?" demanded Molly.

"Because I like Mary Beth better," said Sonny.

"You do?" said Mary Beth in surprise.

Molly couldn't believe it! Mary Beth didn't do nice things for Sonny. She never paid any attention to him at all! How could he like her?

It wasn't fair. Molly felt like crying.

Sonny slipped a valentine card in Mary Beth's pocket as they sang their Pee Wee Scout song. Mary Beth giggled.

Molly couldn't sing. She was trying not to cry. Then she remembered the secret valentines. Someone must like me, she thought. She looked all around the circle. How could she find out?

"See you next Tuesday!" called Mrs. Peters as the Scouts left. Sonny raced off down the street. Molly felt sad. She walked slowly.

When Molly got home, she went to her room. She opened her book bag. Inside was another big white envelope!

A valentine.

A store-bought valentine.

It said, *To Molly* on the outside. Inside, it said:

 Roses are red
Violets are blue
My favorite valentine
Is you, you, you!

Molly flopped on her bed. Oh, boy! She did have a boyfriend after all. She stared at the neat printing. At the bottom it said, *From Kevin.*

Kevin, Kevin, Kevin. A real boyfriend. Her own valentine.

Molly felt like a special Pee Wee Scout.

Pee Wee Scout Song
(to the tune of "Old MacDonald Had a Farm")

Scouts are helpers, Scouts have fun,
Pee Wee, Pee Wee Scouts!
We sing and play when work is done,
Pee Wee, Pee Wee Scouts!

With a good deed here,
And an errand there,
Here a hand, there a hand,
Everywhere a good hand.

Scouts are helpers, Scouts have fun,
Pee Wee, Pee Wee Scouts!

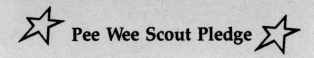 **Pee Wee Scout Pledge**

We love our country
And our home,
Our school and neighbors too.

As Pee Wee Scouts
We pledge our best
In everything we do.